Ellie ✳ Sandall

Follow Me!

h
Hodder
Children's
Books

A division of Hachette Children's Books

First published in 2015 by
Hodder Children's Books

Copyright © Ellie Sandall 2015

Hodder Children's Books
338 Euston Road
London, NW1 3BH

Hodder Children's Books Australia
Level 17/207 Kent Street
Sydney, NSW 2000

The right of Ellie Sandall to be identified as the author and
illustrator of this Work has been asserted by her in accordance
with the Copyright, Designs and Patents Act 1988.

ISBN: 978 1 444 91945 5
10 9 8 7 6 5 4 3 2 1

Printed in China

Hodder Children's Books is a division of
Hachette Children's Books,
an Hachette UK Company

www.hachette.co.uk

It's time to wake up!

Come down from the tree.

Follow me,

follow me,

follow me!

Places to be,

things to do, things to see.

Follow me, follow me, follow me!

things to chase,

Things to hunt,

things to race.

things to scare,

Follow me,

follow me,

follow me!

Things to climb, things to meet,

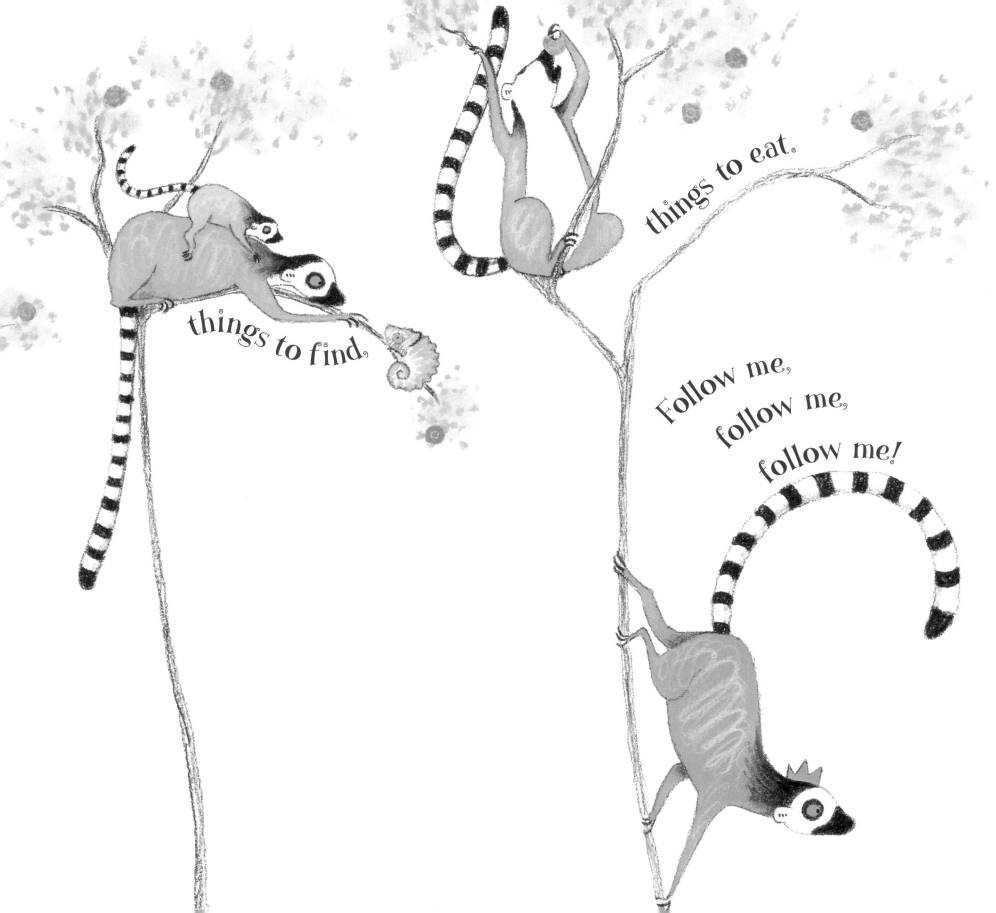

things to find,

things to eat.

Follow me, follow me, follow me!

Things to chew,

things to munch,

things to have
for our lunch.

Follow me,

follow me,

follow me!

Things to jump, things to hop, things to leap, things to...

STOP!

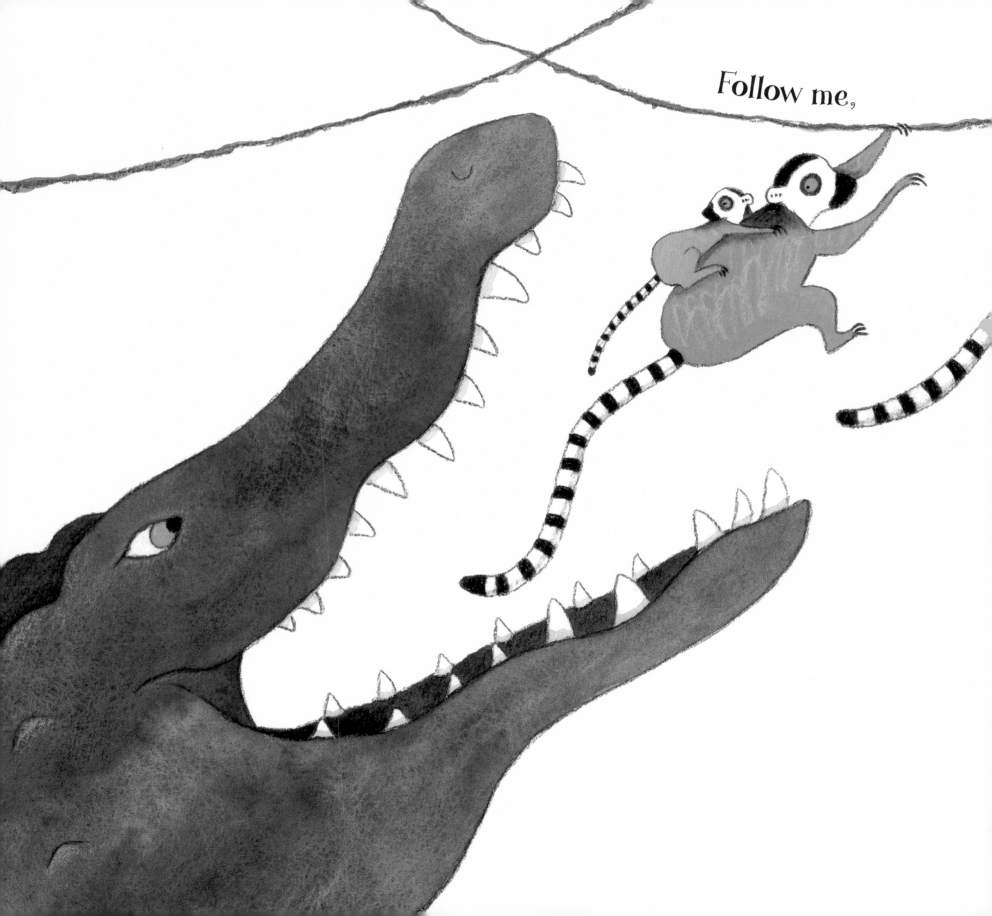

Follow me,

follow me,

follow me!

Phew!

Time to rest, come with me,

back we go to our tree.

Follow me...

follow me...